Write About It

Dona Herweck Rice

Publishing Credits

Rachelle Cracchiolo, M.S.Ed., *Publisher*
Conni Medina, M.A.Ed., *Managing Editor*
Nika Fabienke, Ed.D., *Content Director*
Véronique Bos, *Creative Director*
Shaun N. Bernadou, *Art Director*
Valerie Morales, *Associate Editor*
John Leach, *Assistant Editor*
Courtney Roberson, *Senior Graphic Designer*

Image Credits: All images from iStock and/or Shutterstock.

I0808955

Teacher Created Materials
5301 Oceanus Drive
Huntington Beach, CA 92649-1030
www.tcmpub.com

ISBN 978-1-4938-9848-0

Printed in China
Nordica.082018.CA21800936

They write words

about the  .

snowflakes

They write words

about the  .

snowman

They write words

about the .

bees

They write words

about the .

flowers

They write words

about the .

rocks

They write words

about the  .

grass

They write words

about the  .

tree

They write words

about the  .

leaves

They write words

about the  .

beach

They write words

about the  .

sand

High-Frequency Words

New Words

about
words
write

Review Words

the
they